Hooray for Reading!

For my mom—who made reading an adventure
for hundreds of kids—P. H.

LITTLE SIMON
An imprint of Simon & Schuster Children's Publishing Division
1230 Avenue of the Americas
New York, New York 10020

Manufactured in the United States of America
First Edition
2 4 6 8 10 9 7 5 3 1

Library of Congress Cataloging-in-Publication Data
Hall, Patricia.
Hooray for reading! / by Patricia Hall ; illustrated by Kathryn Mitter.—1st ed.
p. cm.—(Classic Raggedy Ann & Andy) (Ready-to-read)
ISBN 0-689-85206-1 Library Edition
ISBN 0-689-85178-2 Paperback
[1. Reading—Fiction. 2. Dolls—Fiction.] I. Mitter, Kathy, ill. II. Title.
PZ7.H147515 Ho 2002
[E]—dc21
2002000942

CLASSIC
Raggedy Ann & Andy

Hooray for Reading!

by Patricia Hall

illustrated by Kathryn Mitter

Ready-to-Read

Little Simon

New York   London   Toronto   Sydney   Singapore

Marcella came home

from her first day

of school.

She was excited.

"I am learning to read!"

she told Raggedy Ann

and Raggedy Andy.

"Let me show you

how I can read,"

Marcella said.

 6

She sat her dolls in rows.

Then she held up cards.

"**Apple**," said Marcella,

"and **Ant**."

 8

These words begin with **A**."

Marcella held up

two more cards.

 10

"**Baby** and **Ball**," she said.

"These are **B** words."

Marcella held up more cards.

She read more words.

"Isn't learning to read fun?"

asked Marcella.

Then she went outside to play.

"Did you hear?"

asked Cleety the Clown.

"She knew all the words!"

said Frederika.

 14

"Marcella is very smart!"

said the Camel

with the Wrinkled Knees.

"Reading is an adventure,"

said Raggedy Ann,

"I love to read."

"I love adventures!"

said Raggedy Andy.

"Can you help us

learn to read, Raggedy Ann?"

the dolls asked.

Raggedy Ann found a crayon.

She drew on some cards.

"Take your seats,"

she said.

"School is starting!"

Raggedy Ann held two cards.

"Here are two **A** words,"

she said.

"Here are words

that start with **B.**

Bunny and **Brown Bear**!"

said Eddie Elephant.

"Look what begins with **C**!"

said Raggedy Ann.

"**Camel**!" giggled Uncle Clem.

"**Clem**!" laughed

the Camel with the Wrinkled Knees.

"How about some **D** words?"

asked Raggedy Ann.

"**Doll, Duck,** and **Danny**

Daddles!" said Frederika.

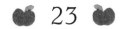 23

"Here come some **E** words!"

sang Raggedy Ann.

"**Eddie** and **Elephant**!"

said Raggedy Andy.

"What begins with **F**?"

asked Raggedy Ann.

"**Fido**!"

laughed Raggedy Andy.

"And **Frederika**, too!"

"Hooray for reading!"

But then—

Blump! Clump! Blump!

The dolls fell off the bed

and the cards flew

everywhere!

"Oh, my," sighed Uncle Clem.

"Learning to read

is an adventure!"

"And a mess,"

said Raggedy Andy.

"Don't worry,"

said Raggedy Ann.

"We know our alphabet now.

We can stack the cards

by their letters."

Soon the playroom

was neat again.

Then in came Marcella.

"Today we read

a **real** book at school!"

she said.

"It was an **adventure** story!"

"You cannot **really** read,"

said Marcella.

"But maybe someday—

you can have

a reading adventure too!"